L.O.L. Surprise! : Secrets and Dreams Journal
A CENTUM BOOK 978-1-4998-1078-3

Distributed by

an imprint of Little Bee Books

251 Park Avenue South, New York, NY, 10010
BuzzPop and associated colophon are trademarks of Little Bee Books.

buzzpopbooks.com

Published in Great Britain by Centum Books Ltd.
This edition published 2019.
1 3 5 7 9 10 8 6 4 2

For information about special discounts on bulk purchases, please contact
Little Bee Books at sales@littlebeebooks.com.

Centum Books Ltd, 20 Devon Square, Newton Abbot, Devon, TQ12 2HR, UK

books@centumbooksltd.co.uk

CENTUM BOOKS Limited Reg. No. 07641486

Printed in the United States of America LSC 0119

KEEP YOUR SECRETS, FOLLOW YOUR DREAMS!

Hi bae,

YOUR L.O.L. BFFs KNOW THE IMPORTANCE OF KEEPING YOUR SECRETS, SECRET. THEY ALSO BELIEVE THAT IF YOU CAN DREAM IT, **YOU CAN DO IT!** THAT'S WHY THEY'VE CREATED THIS CRAZY-CUTE JOURNAL FOR YOU TO RECORD YOUR DEEPEST SECRETS AND WILDEST DREAMS. **EXCITED YET?** INSIDE, YOU'LL FIND EVERYTHING YOU NEED TO KEEP YOUR SECRETS SAFE. ARE YOU GOOD AT KEEPING SECRETS? TAKE THE QUIZ ON PAGE 24 TO FIND OUT. NEED TO WRITE A TOP SECRET NOTE TO YOUR BFF? PICK SOME NOTEPAPER FROM PAGE 80 ONWARDS AND FOLLOW THE INSTRUCTIONS TO CREATE AN ORIGAMI MASTERPIECE. PLUS, YOU CAN WRITE A LETTER TO YOUR FUTURE SELF ON PAGE 76, COMPLETE A DREAM DIARY ON PAGE 18, AND USE THE INSTRUCTIONS ON PAGE 36 TO MAKE YOUR OWN DARLING DREAM CATCHER. EVERYTHING YOU NEED TO MAKE YOUR **DREAMS COME TRUE!** THE L.O.L. BABES CAN'T WAIT TO HELP YOU KEEP YOUR SECRETS AND FOLLOW YOUR DREAMS. SO, ARE YOU READY, B.B.?

Bling it on!

Contents

Page 10 — QUIZ: ARE YOU A DREAMER OR A DOER?

Page 12 — D.I.Y. SECRET KEEPER

Page 20 — DREAM DECODER

Page 40 — SECRET SELFIES

Page 54 — SECRET TEXTS

Page 60 — CREATE A PURR-FECT PAL FOR THE LIL REBELS TO ADOPT.

Page 71 — MY BUCKET LIST

© MGA

IT'S A SECRET

This journal is made especially for you to share your most important secrets. But secrets should be kept just that: secret! Create your own alphabet code so the secrets you write in this book are kept confidential.

Step 1:

Start by choosing a letter, number or symbol to represent each letter in the alphabet. For example, you could use numbers from 1 to 26 for each letter, so "A" becomes 1, "B" becomes 2, "C" becomes 3, and so on. Then, your code would look a little like this. …

A	B	C	D	E	F	G	H	I	J
1	2	3	4	5	6	7	8	9	10

K	L	M	N	O	P	Q	R	S	T
11	12	13	14	15	16	17	18	19	20

U	V	W	X	Y	Z
21	22	23	24	25	26

Step 2:

Next, start writing your secret using the code. Here's an example using the number code above:

I LOVE L.O.L.

becomes

9 12-15-22-5 12-15-12

Step 3:

If you're sharing your secret with someone else, make sure you give them a copy of the code, too. That way, they'll be able to decode your message themselves.

Now it's your turn....

Fill in the boxes below each letter with your chosen numbers, letters or symbols. Grab a piece of paper and practice writing in your code. Try testing out different types of code, too. The trickier, the better!

A	B	C	D	E	F	G	H	I	J

K	L	M	N	O	P	Q	R	S	T

U	V	W	X	Y	Z

© MGA

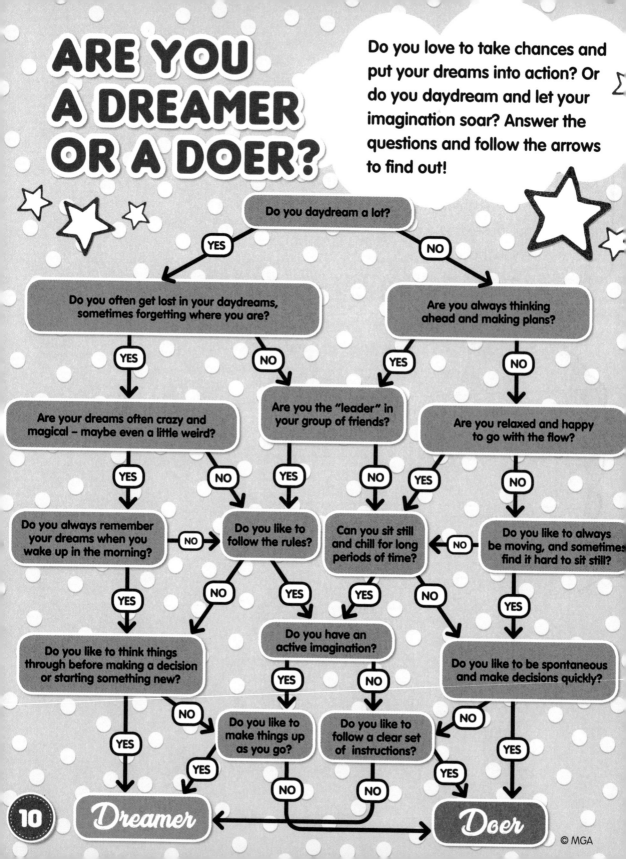

ARE YOU A DREAMER OR A DOER?

Do you love to take chances and put your dreams into action? Or do you daydream and let your imagination soar? Answer the questions and follow the arrows to find out!

Do you daydream a lot?

YES

NO

Do you often get lost in your daydreams, sometimes forgetting where you are?

Are you always thinking ahead and making plans?

YES — Are your dreams often crazy and magical – maybe even a little weird?

NO — Are you the "leader" in your group of friends?

YES — (to Are you the "leader"...)

NO — Are you relaxed and happy to go with the flow?

YES — Do you always remember your dreams when you wake up in the morning?

NO — Do you like to follow the rules?

YES — (Do you like to follow the rules?)

Can you sit still and chill for long periods of time?

NO ← (from) Do you like to always be moving, and sometimes find it hard to sit still?

YES (Do you always remember your dreams) — Do you like to think things through before making a decision or starting something new?

NO → (Do you like to follow the rules?)

Do you have an active imagination?

YES — Do you like to make things up as you go?

NO — Do you like to follow a clear set of instructions?

Do you like to be spontaneous and make decisions quickly?

NO → (to Do you like to follow a clear set of instructions?)

YES → **Doer**

YES (Do you like to think things through) → **Dreamer**

NO → (Do you like to make things up as you go?)

YES (make things up) → **Dreamer**

NO → **Doer**

YES (follow a clear set of instructions?) → **Doer**

NO → **Dreamer**

Dreamer

Doer

Dreamer

You're calm and relaxed, with a curious mind and a great imagination. You can often be found daydreaming away, bursting with creative ideas. Keep dreaming big, B.B.! But don't forget – if you can dream it, you can do it. So, remember to get out there and put those dreams into action. The L.O.L. babes have your back, and they believe in you!

Doer

You're a superactive B.B. who loves putting plans into action. You're always busy working on something special, and once that's finished, you're looking for your next big project! Decision-making comes naturally to you, and you like to move fast to get the job done. But remember – taking time to chill out and slow down can be great for creativity. So, kick back, relax and let the ideas flow!

11

D.I.Y. SECRET KEEPER

It's amazing how much can change in a year. Think back to one year ago – what's changed for you since then? Do you still have the same crush, the same fears, the same secrets? Well, PhD B.B. would like to perform a little experiment! Are you ready? Let's go!

Steps:

1. Ask an adult to help you cut out the hearts on the opposite page.

2. Write your answers to the questions on the back of each of the hearts.

3. Turn to page 15 and cut along the dotted lines, so you're left with a square piece of paper.

4. Follow the instructions on the paper to make your envelope.

5. Seal the envelope with glue, and then fill in the information on the front. PhD B.B. suggests choosing a date that is exactly one year from today – but it's totally up to you!

6. Hide the envelope somewhere safe, but make sure it's in a place you will remember!

7. Leave the envelope in your hiding place and wait to open it on the date you've chosen.

8. Once opened, answer the questions on page 17 of this book to find out what's changed about you!

YOU WILL NEED:
Scissors
Pen or pencil
Glue stick

REMEMBER!
ASK AN ADULT TO HELP YOU

CUT HERE!

WHO IS YOUR BFF?

WHO IS YOUR SECRET CRUSH?

WHAT ARE YOU MOST AFRAID OF?

WHAT IS YOUR MOST SECRET WISH?

WHAT'S YOUR BIG DREAM FOR THE FUTURE?

WHAT'S YOUR MOST EMBARRASSING MOMENT?

13

D.I.Y. ENVELOPE

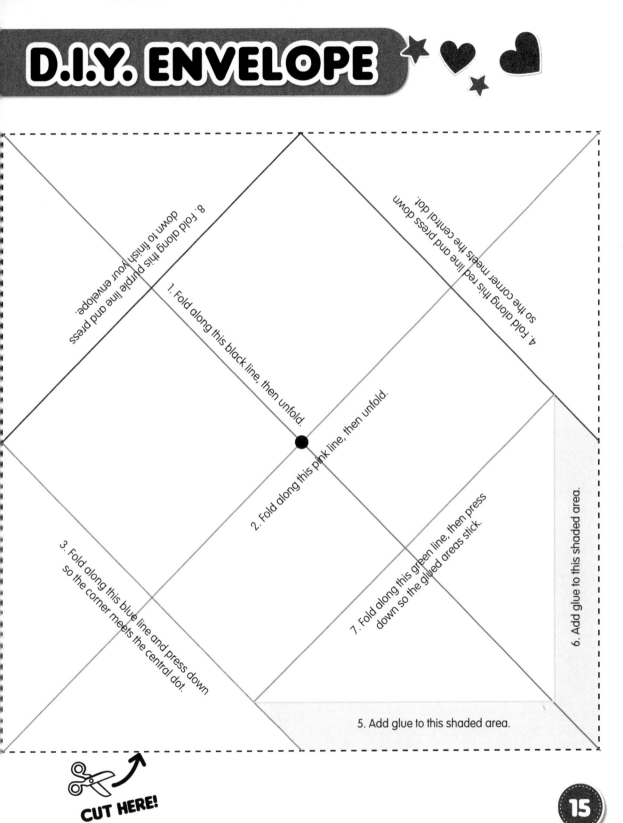

4. Fold along this red line and press down so the corner meets the central dot.

8. Fold along this purple line and press down to finish your envelope.

1. Fold along this black line, then unfold.

2. Fold along this pink line, then unfold.

3. Fold along this blue line and press down so the corner meets the central dot.

7. Fold along this green line, then press down so the glued areas stick.

6. Add glue to this shaded area.

5. Add glue to this shaded area.

CUT HERE!

15

TOP SECRET!

Open me in one year on the _____ of _____ 20_____.

For _____ 's eyes only.

© MGA

ONE YEAR LATER ...

Okay, B.B. The time has come! Open your secret envelope, read your one-year-old secrets and then answer the questions below.

Are you and your bestie still BFFs?

....

....

....

Do you still have a secret crush on the same person? If not, who's your new crush?

....

....

....

Are you still afraid of the same things? If so, write down ways you can conquer your fears.

....

....

....

Do you still have the same secret wish? If not, what do you wish for now?

....

....

....

Are you still embarrassed about your most embarrassing moment?

....

....

....

Is your big dream for the future still the same, or has it changed?

....

....

MY DREAM DIARY

Dreams are like secret stories told to you while you sleep, and they can reveal a lot about what you're thinking. Use these pages to write down your dreams every day for one week. Keep this book and a pen beside your bed and write down your dreams as soon as you wake up.

Monday

Tuesday

Wednesday

Thursday

Friday

Saturday

Sunday

DREAM DECODER

Now that the week is finished, it's time to explore your dreams! Complete the checklists below to find out what secrets your dreams are trying to tell you.

My dreams were mostly ...
- Funny
- Weird
- Scary
- Magical
- Mysterious
- Boring
- Realistic
- Happy

I was usually ...
- Running
- Eating
- Swimming
- Dancing
- Singing
- Flying
- Walking
- Laughing

I was usually with ...
- Friends
- Family
- Strangers
- Celebrities
- Animals
- Aliens
- My L.O.L. dolls
- No one

My dreams mostly took place ...
- At home
- At school
- At a friend's house
- In space
- Under the sea
- In a movie or TV show
- Onstage
- In another country

CHECK OFF THE STARS!

When I woke up, remembering my dreams was ...
- Supereasy, I could remember every detail.
- A little difficult. I had to really think about it.
- So hard! I could only remember a few details.
- Impossible, I couldn't remember a thing!

20

What do your dreams mean?

Flying

Dreams about flying can be the best kind because they often represent freedom, joy and happiness! They might also mean that you have worked your way out of a sticky situation in real life. Nice one, B.B.!

Running

Dreams where you are running away from something might mean you're worried about an event in real life. Have you got a big test, game or performance coming up? Think about what it could be, find your courage, and tackle it head-on. You can do it, B.B.!

Animals

When you dream about animals, they can often represent people you know. The type of animal a person becomes in your dream might be your brain's way of revealing how you see them in real life.

Travel

Dreams about travelling – like on a plane, car, bus, boat or spaceship – can be your brain's way of telling you to move forward and try new things. Have you been thinking of joining a new team, trying that new dance move or experimenting with a new style? Now's your time to shine!

Top tips for remembering your dreams:

1. Be quick!

The details of your dream will start to fade away as the day goes on. So, write down your dreams as soon as you wake up.

2. Stay ready

Always keep a pen and notebook beside your bed.

3. Get a good night's sleep

Allow yourself 30 minutes before bedtime to relax and wind down. That means no TV, computer or phone time before bed!

Baby Next Door wants to know what you're thinking! Write down the first things that pop into your head. Keep writing until the thought bubble is full.

Ready, steady, go!

© MGA

YOU WILL NEED:

- 1 bowl
- 2 cotton balls
- ¼ cup of baking soda
- ¼ cup of water
- ¼ cup of grape or cranberry juice (or any dark-colored juice)
- White paper

REMEMBER!
ASK AN ADULT TO HELP YOU

MAKE YOUR OWN MAGIC INK

Looking for a superstealthy way to write secret notes to your BFFs? Follow the instructions below to create a batch of your very own invisible ink.

2 FLY 4 WORDS!

Steps:

1. Ask an adult to help you add the water and baking soda to a bowl, and then mix them together.

2. Dip one cotton ball into the mixture.

3. Use the cotton ball to write your message on the paper.

4. Wait until the ink is completely dry.

5. Dip another cotton ball into the juice.

6. Paint the juice over your message and wait for it to appear – just like magic!

23

© MGA

ARE YOU GOOD AT KEEPING SECRETS?

Do you always keep secrets under lock and key, or do you sometimes let them slip? Take this quiz to find out!

1. When a friend tells you a secret, you …

A) Keep it to myself, of course! Secrets are safe with me.

B) I might tell one or two of my other BFFs, but only the most trustworthy ones!

C) Tell anyone who will listen, especially if it's something juicy! Some secrets are too good not to share.

2. You're with your BFF when they have a superembarrassing moment. What do you do?

A) Keep it between us, so they don't feel embarrassed in front of anyone else. That's what friends are for!

B) If it was a superfunny moment then I might spill to another BFF. Everyone likes a giggle!

C) OMG, I literally can't keep something that funny to myself! I'd just *have* to share it with our other BFFs, too.

3. Your BFF tells you a secret that they should really tell their parents, too. You …

A) Tell no one. A secret's a secret! Loyalty comes first.

B) Tell one other friend, so we can share the worry and help our friend together.

C) Tell their parents straightaway. No secret is worth keeping if it means my BFF might be in trouble.

4. A friend starts telling you someone else's secret. What do you do?

A) Ask them to stop! I don't want to hear secrets I'm not supposed to know.

B) Ask them if the other friend won't mind them sharing, or if there's a good reason for them to be telling me.

C) Listen in, B.B. Everyone likes a little gossip!

5. How does it make you feel when a friend tells you a secret?

A) Superspecial! It means a lot that they trust me. I won't tell anyone!

B) Understanding, but a little nervous. I'll do my best to keep their secret safe.

C) Ugh, terrible! I hate being asked to keep secrets. I find it so hard not to spill!

24

MOSTLY As - Superhero secret keeper

You're a superloyal BFF! Your friends know their secrets are always safe with you. You know the importance of being a trustworthy friend, and you'll never spill a secret – no matter what it is. But remember: It's okay to tell a secret to a parent or grown-up if you think a friend might be hurt or in trouble. Looking out for your BFF always comes first!

Top Tip

KEEPING SECRETS CAN BE A BIG RESPONSIBILITY. USE A DIARY, OR THIS JOURNAL, TO WRITE DOWN SECRETS WHEN THEY GET TOO HEAVY TO CARRY. THAT WAY, YOU CAN VENT YOUR FEELINGS WHILE STILL STAYING LOYAL TO YOUR BESTIES.

MOSTLY Bs - Somewhere in-between

You always do your best to keep secrets, but sometimes you can't help but let them slip! However, you only ever share secrets with your most trustworthy BFFs, and you never indulge in gossip. This makes you a great friend! But even your most trusted BFF might have another friend that they share secrets with, too. So, keep this in mind next time you share a friend's secret – it might be better to keep it safe instead.

MOSTLY Cs - Secret spiller

You're a great talker – and a bit of a gossip! – who loves to chat and giggle with friends. Secret keeping is not your best skill, and you're known to let things slip. Sharing embarrassing moments can be funny, but make sure you're always laughing with your friends, never at them. And it's okay to let your BFF know if you find it hard to keep secrets under wraps. That way you're still being totally honest, which is what being BFFs is all about!

25

RIDDLE ME THIS!

We all know M.C. Swag loves to rhyme, but did you know she can riddle, too? Solve the riddles below to reveal secrets about some of your L.O.L. pals. Turn this page upside down to check your answers.

A. Her dress is black on one side, but what's on the other? If you name it, you'll know Heartbreaker's favorite color.

Heartbreaker's favorite color is …

_____

B. Full of stars and planets and the Milky Way is the place where Glamstronaut would like to go someday.

Glamstronaut would like to go …

_____

26

© MGA

USE THIS PAGE TO WRITE YOUR OWN RIDDLES AS A FUN WAY TO REVEAL SECRETS TO YOUR BFFS.

IN MY WILDEST DREAMS ...

Sometimes our dreams can be wacky, crazy and a lil' outrageous!
Use these pages to draw or write about your weirdest, wildest dreams.

MY DREAM CAREER

What do you dream of doing when you grow up? Maybe you'd like to be a zookeeper, a scientist or a painter? Boss Queen believes that if you can dream it, you can do it! Fill in these pages to start putting your big dreams into action.

If I could have any job in the world, it would be …

....

....

I'm really good at …

....

....

In my dream job, I would be …

♡ Working as part of a team. Teamwork makes the dream work!

♡ Leading a team. I wanna be the boss, B.B.!

♡ Working solo. I like to be independent.

In order to get my dream job, I'll need to learn how to …

....

....

I want to be able to …

- ♡ Help others
- ♡ Help animals
- ♡ Be creative
- ♡ Be active
- ♡ Solve problems
- ♡ Make big decisions

YOU BETTA WERK!

A job I definitely don't want to do is …

....

....

Someone I really look up to is …

....

....

Because …

....

....

In my dream job, I hope to …

- ♡ Change the world
- ♡ Create amazing things
- ♡ Achieve the impossible
- ♡ Inspire others
- ♡ Share knowledge
- ♡ All of the above!

31

© MGA

WE'RE GOING ON A TREASURE HUNT!

Not only is a sleepover the perfect time for telling secrets and dreaming big, it's also the best time to play fun games with your BFFs! Next time you're at a sleepover, practice your clue-solving skills with this secret treasure hunt game.

YOU WILL NEED:

- A few pens or pencils
- Paper, cut into postcard-sized pieces
- One L.O.L. doll or another toy or item of your choice
- Your BFFs!

TAG! UR IT!

Aim of the game:

Write fun clues for your friends to follow, eventually leading them to discover a hidden surprise!

How to play:

1. Hide your L.O.L. doll (or another item) somewhere secret inside your house, or outside in the yard. Make sure your friends don't see you. No peeking allowed!

2. Write clues on pieces of paper and leave them scattered around the house and yard for your friends to find. Hand your friends the first clue to get them started! Each clue should lead to the next one, with the last clue leading to your hidden doll or item.

3. Once your friends have found the hidden surprise, it's your turn to follow the clues! Choose another friend to hide a new surprise and start again.

© MGA

Writing clues is superfun, but it can be a little tricky at first. Here are a few examples to get you started. Your clues don't have to rhyme, but choosing rhyming words can be a great challenge!

For example:

Perhaps you'll hide your first clue in the yard outside …

OUTSIDE WHERE THE FLOWERS GROW, YOU'LL FIND A CLUE THAT WILL TELL YOU WHERE TO GO.

Then the clue hidden in the yard leads you past a swing set and under a tree …

ALONG THE PATH AND AROUND THE SWING, YOUR NEXT CLUE HIDES UNDER A BIG GREEN THING!

GO INSIDE THE HOUSE NOW, IT'S TIME FOR BED. THERE'S A SURPRISE HIDDEN WHERE I REST MY HEAD.

And finally, the clue under the tree leads to your hidden surprise, which is back inside the house and underneath your pillow!

33

PINKY PROMISE!

Sharing dreams, secrets and stories is what friendship is all about. Grab your most trusted BFF, fill in the info below, and make a pinky promise to always keep each other's secrets.

#SQUAD goals

Don't forget to sign!

STICK A PHOTO OF YOU AND YOUR BFF HERE!

I _____ promise
(Write your name here)

to be a loyal BFF and always keep

_____ 's secrets.
(Write your BFF's name here)

Signed:

_____
(Your autograph, please!)

© MGA

STICK A PHOTO OF YOU
AND YOUR BFF HERE!

I _____ promise
(Write your name here)

to be a loyal BFF and always keep

_____ 's secrets.
(Write your BFF's name here)

Signed:

_____
(Your autograph, please!)

SHINE BRIGHT

© MGA

© MGA

D.I.Y. DREAM CATCHER

A dream catcher is not only a great way to ward off bad dreams, it's also a super-adorbs addition to your bedroom! Follow the instructions below to make your very own dream catcher.

Top Tip

MAKE SURE YOU ASK AN ADULT TO HELP YOU BEFORE BEGINNING YOUR DREAM CATCHER.

Steps:

1. Choose six craft sticks and as many wooden beads as you like and paint them different colors. Try matching your colors to the cutouts on the opposite page.

2. While your beads and craft sticks are drying, cut out the shapes on the opposite page. Use the tip of a pen or pencil to push a hole through the white spot on each shape.

3. Cut three different length pieces of yarn (one for each shape).

4. Thread one piece through the hole in each shape and tie a few knots at the end to stop the shape from falling off.

5. Once your beads are dry, thread a few onto the end of each piece of yarn so they sit just on top of the shape.

6. Once your craft sticks are dry, ask an adult to glue the ends of each stick together to form a six-sided hexagon.

7. Once the glue is dry, you're ready to make your web. The web is the part that catches all the bad dreams. Cut a long piece of yarn and tie one end to one of the craft sticks. Wrap it back and forth around the center of the hexagon, then tie with a knot.

8. Repeat step 7 with as many more pieces of yarn as you like. You could also try stringing a bead or two onto one of the pieces to add some extra color to your web.

9. Grab the yarn with the shapes and beads and tie them onto your hexagon.

10. Hang your dream catcher above your bed and let the good dreams roll!

CUT HERE!

© MGA

DREAM ON, DREAMER!

What do you think Sleepy Bones is dreaming about? Draw her dreams below.

© MGA

SECRET SELFIES

Everybody loves a selfie, and selfies are even better with dress-ups! Ask an adult to help you cut out the selfie props on the opposite page, then grab your BFFs and strike a pose! When you've found the perfect pics, print them out and stick them in below.

Don't forget to add a cute hashtag!

STICK YOUR
SELFIE HERE!

REMEMBER!
ASK AN ADULT
TO HELP YOU

STICK YOUR
SELFIE HERE!

#..

#..

CUT HERE!

41

© MGA

42

EYE SPY

Have you got what it takes to be a superspy? Pick your secret identity and fill in your mission details below.

CHOCOLATE MILK. SHAKEN, NOT STIRRED.

My code name is ....

My superspy skills are ....

My top secret mission is ....

My trustworthy spy partner is ....

Our mission will take place in ....

We will need assistance from our fellow L.O.L. Surprise! secret agents. Their names are:

....

....

....

IT'S CLASSY-FIED!

Every secret agent must keep supersecret files! Using your code from page eight, write down all the top secret info from your recent mission.

TOP SECRET

WRITE YOUR NOTES HERE!

TOP SECRET

DREAM IT. DO IT!

You've already written about your career dreams, now it's time to focus on your other big dreams! Maybe you'd like to improve your soccer skills, write a book, or learn to surf? Write about them below. Remember, dreaming of the "future" doesn't always mean thinking years ahead. You might have a big goal to achieve next week, next month or next year!

EAT. SLEEP. BEACH.

My big dream is ...

To achieve it, I'll need to ...

My big dream is ...

To achieve it, I'll need to ...

My big dream is ...

....

....

To achieve it, I'll need to ...

....

....

My big dream is ...

....

....

To achieve it, I'll need to ...

....

....

My big dream is ...

....

....

To achieve it, I'll need to ...

....

....

SECRET MESSAGES

How are your secret message-solving skills? See if you can decode the messages below. You may recognize these from the messages found inside your L.O.L. Surprise! Turn this page upside down to check your answers.

L.O.L. SURPRISE!
©MGA
TROPHY WINNER

=
_____

L.O.L. SURPRISE!
©MGA
SHINE BRIGHT LIKE A DIAMOND

=
_____

L.O.L. SURPRISE!
©MGA
FANGIRL

=
_____

L.O.L. SURPRISE!
©MGA
SICK BEAT

=
_____

© MGA

Now it's your turn to create your own secret messages!

Cut out the mini pictures and add them to the spaces below in different combinations. Then, ask your BFFs to solve them!

MAKE SURE YOU COMPLETE THE ACTIVITY ON PAGES 50-51 BEFORE CUTTING OUT YOUR MINI PICTURES.

✂ **CUT HERE!**

☐ **+** ☐ **=** _____

☐ **+** ☐ **=** _____

☐ **+** ☐ **=** _____

☐ **+** ☐ **=** _____

☐ **+** ☐ **=** _____

TIME TO SPILL!

A good secret keeper never spills a secret! But sometimes writing secrets down helps to take the weight off your shoulders. Fill in the questions using your secret code, or hide this book to keep your secrets extrasafe.

OUTTA SIGHT, B.B.!

My biggest secret is ...

The biggest secret I've ever spilled was ...

The longest time I've kept someone else's secret is ...

50

© MGA

The funniest secret I've ever been told is …

The most embarrassing secret I know is …

One secret I really want to spill, but can't, is …

One secret I'll never spill is …

MY DREAM HOME

If you could design and create your dream home, what would it look like and where would it be? Fill in these pages to start planning your home sweet home.

I'd love to live ...
- ⭐ By the sea
- ⭐ In the forest
- ⭐ In the mountains
- ⭐ By a river
- ⭐ In a city
- ⭐ In a village
- ⭐ On an island
- ⭐ In the snow

If I could live anywhere in the world, it would be ...

- -

I would share my dream home with ...

- -

The best thing about my dream home would be ...

- -

WON'T U B MY NEIGHBOR?

My dream home would have to have a ...
- ⭐ Pool
- ⭐ Spa
- ⭐ Fireplace
- ⭐ Tennis court
- ⭐ Gym
- ⭐ Movie theater
- ⭐ Library
- ⭐ Music studio

My dream home would have to be ...
- ⭐ Small and cute
- ⭐ Big and spacious
- ⭐ Warm and cozy
- ⭐ Light and airy

Decode your message here.

_____

_____

_____

_____

_____

_____

_____

_____

_____

_____

_____

_____

WANDERLUST DREAMS

The L.O.L. babes are always ready for an adventure! Use these pages to write all about your dream vacation. Dream big, B.B., and get ready to inspire some serious #TravelEnvy.

The country I've always dreamed of visiting is ...

....

Because ...

....

....

I've always wanted to see the ...

- ♡ Eiffel Tower
- ♡ Pyramids of Giza
- ♡ Taj Mahal
- ♡ Grand Canyon
- ♡ Great Barrier Reef
- ♡ Stonehenge
- ♡ Great Wall of China
- ♡ Leaning Tower of Pisa
- ♡ Mount Everest

STICK YOUR PHOTO HERE!

Draw a picture or stick in a photo of your dream destination here.

The L.O.L. Surprise! doll I would take with me on my travels is …

....

We'd make great travel partners because …

....

My dream adventure would involve lots of …

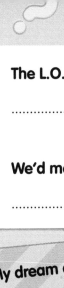

♡ Swimming in the sea

♡ Relaxing by the pool

♡ Hiking in the mountains

♡ Skiing in the snow

♡ Camping in the forest

♡ Searching for wild animals

♡ Exploring in the city

♡ Eating delicious food

♡ Meeting new people

*For my dream adventure,
I'd need to pack …*

_____

_____

_____

_____

_____

I hope to return home from my adventure feeling …

....

57

GIMME THAT GLITTER

The Glitterati gurls' outfits are always on point.
Design new accessories for these glamorous babes.

WHAT'S THE BUZZ, HONEY?

PURR-FECTION!

BORN TO BE STARS

The lil' rebels are all about living your best life and being whoever you want to be. Fill in these future predictions about you and your fab friends.

The friend most likely to win gold at the Olympics is

....

They've got serious sports skills.

The friend most likely to become a superstar singer is

....

Their voice is beautiful.

The friend most likely to become a fashion icon is

....

They can make anything stylish!

The friend most likely to invent something amazing is

....

They're supersmart.

The friend most likely to write the next best seller is

....

Everything they write is incredible.

The friend most likely to become a stage sensation is

....

Acting is their passion.

59

MEOW! WOOF! SQUEAK!

The L.O.L. Surprise! pets are just as cute 'n' sassy as their doll BFFs. Design a new purr-fect pal for the tots to adopt.

DRAW YOUR PET HERE!

DON'T FORGET THEIR AWESOME ACCESSORIES

GIVE THEM A CUTE QUOTE

DESIGN A BEAUT BOTTLE FOR THEM

SASS 'N' SMARTS

LAB IS FAB!

The S.T.E.M. Club love to discover and invent.
Design a cool new gadget for them to build.

Name your
gadget: _____

Draw your gadget here:

What is it used for?

_____

_____

_____

_____

_____

IF IT AIN'T
BROKE, DON'T
FIX IT!

L.O.L. SECRETS

Goo Goo Queen, Touchdown and Grunge Grrrl each have a secret to share with you. What do you think they are? Make up sweet secrets for each L.O.L. babe and write them below.

Goo Goo Queen's secret is ...

_____

_____

Touchdown's secret is ...

_____

_____

_____

Grunge Grrrl's secret is …

_____

_____

_____

Now pick your fave lil rebel, draw her below and give her a secret, too.

(write your lil rebel's name here)

_____

_____ 's secret is …

_____

_____

_____

63

© MGA

MY DREAM STYLE

Is there an outfit or accessory you've been dreaming of trying out? Remember that fashion is all about wearing what makes you happy and comfortable. So, if you've been waiting to kick it in those new kicks or rock that '80s look, now is your time to shine! Use these pages to write all about your dream style.

I would describe my style as ...

♥ Glam

♥ Edgy

♥ Cool

♥ Classic

♥ Retro

♥ Cute

♥ Funky

♥ Sporty

To me, style is all about ...

....
....
....
....
....

My style inspiration is ...

Because ...

....

My dream style looks like ...

DRAW OR STICK IN PICTURES OF YOUR DREAM STYLE. WILL YOU GO FOR THE RETRO GLAM OF THE PAST LIKE '80s B.B. OR FUTURISTIC FAB LIKE VR Q.T.? BE CREATIVE AND A LIL' OUTRAGEOUS!

IT'S A DREAM COME TRUE

You've got a dream catcher to catch those spooky dreams, now you need something to make your good dreams come true! Follow Genie's instructions to make your very own dream mobile to hang above your bed.

Steps:

1. Cut out the hearts on the opposite page.

2. On the back of each heart, write a dream that you would like to come true.

3. Cut five different length pieces of twine.

4. Thread the needle with a long length of twine and sew through the top of one of the hearts. Tie a bow at the end to stop the heart from falling off.

5. Ask an adult to help you push the needle through the straw (try not to bend it as you go).

6. Thread the twine through the straw and decide how low you want the heart to hang below it. Then tie a double knot in the twine above the straw and trim.

7. Repeat steps 4 – 6 with the rest of the hearts. Hang each heart at a different length.

8. Cut a length of twine about 1.5 ft long, thread it through the straw at both ends and tie a knot at each end to secure it. This creates your hanging loop.

9. Hang above your bed and wait for your dreams to come true!

Top Tip

MAKE SURE YOU ASK AN ADULT TO HELP YOU BEFORE BEGINNING YOUR DREAM MOBILE.

CUT HERE!

© MGA

© MGA

CUT HERE!

REMEMBER!
ASK AN ADULT
TO HELP YOU

Shh! Dreaming
in progress.

© MGA

Daydreaming away ...

© MGA

MY BUCKET LIST

A bucket list is a list of things that you just HAVE to do, try or see one day. Bucket list items are superspecial, once-in-a-lifetime things – so dream big, B.B.! Every time you think of something new you'd love to do, try or see, write it here.

ONE GIANT LEAP FOR BABYKIND!

MY DREAM PET

Animals make amazing friends! Imagine if you could have any animal – real or magical – as your pet BFF. Your adventures would be totally wild! Dream up your fur-bulous new friend below.

My favorite real pet is a ...

- Dog
- Cat
- Horse
- Hamster
- Rabbit
- Fish
- Turtle
- Bird

My favorite imaginary pet is a ...

- Unicorn
- Dragon
- Sea monster
- Pegasus
- Griffin
- Phoenix

My favorite L.O.L. pet is ...

If I could have any animal as a pet, it would be a ...

....
....

Because ...

....
....

Its name would be ...

....
....

Its favorite snack would be ...

....
....

DRAW OR STICK IN A PICTURE OF YOUR DREAM PET. TRY MAKING A COLLAGE OF DIFFERENT PICTURES - THAT WAY YOU CAN CREATE SOMETHING WITH THE BODY OF A LION, THE WINGS OF A BIRD AND THE HORN OF A UNICORN!

TRUST ME!

Bling Queen and '80s B.B. know that keeping and sharing secrets is all about trust! Have you and your BFF got what it takes? Try these fun games together to build trust and strengthen your friendship.

#1 Trust fall

Stand in front of your BFF with your back to them. Make sure you're close enough that they're able to place their palms flat on your back. Ask your BFF to stand with their arms stretched out, ready to catch you. Close your eyes and slowly fall backwards. As you do, your BFF will catch you in their arms. Now swap places and start again!

#2 Trust walk

Find a piece of material or clothing and tie it around your head so it covers your eyes like a blindfold. You should not be able to see through it. Ask your BFF to take your hand and lead you along a path around the house or yard, telling you where to go, when to turn and when to stop. Once you reach the end, swap places and start again.

#3 Draw a twin

Grab a pen and a piece of paper. Draw a picture of something – maybe a person, a tiger or a flower – without letting your BFF see. Without showing them your drawing, give instructions to your BFF to draw the same picture without telling them what it is. For example, if you have drawn a house, you can tell your BFF to draw a square (for the building) and then a triangle on top (for the roof). Once you've finished, compare your two drawings. How similar are they?

#4 Two truths and a lie

We all know you would never lie to your BFF IRL! But if you make an exception for this game, it can be a great way to work out how well you know each other. Tell your BFF three things about yourself: two true and one false. Then, ask your BFF to guess which two things are true and which one is a lie. How well did your BFF do? Now swap places and start again.

TO MY FUTURE FAB SELF ...

If you could time travel into the future, what would you have hoped to achieve by then? Write a letter to your future self, listing all your amazing dreams and goals.

Dear .... year old .... ,

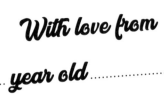

With love from

.... year old ....

Ask an adult to cut out your letter. Then, make the envelope on the opposite page, put your letter inside it and keep it somewhere safe. Open the letter when you reach a certain age – maybe 12, 18 or 25 years old – and see what amazing things you've achieved!

D.I.Y. ENVELOPE

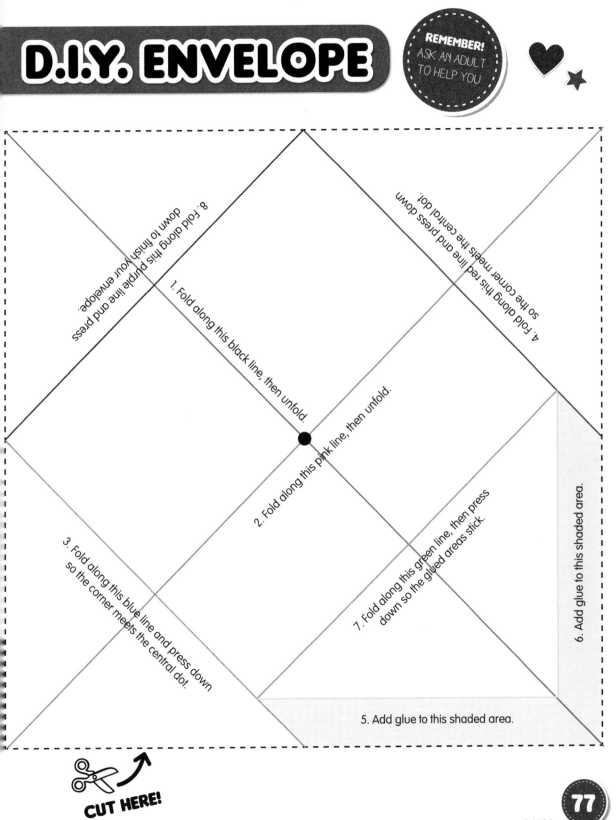

8. Fold along this purple line and press down to finish your envelope.

4. Fold along this red line and press down so the corner meets the central dot.

1. Fold along this black line, then unfold.

2. Fold along this pink line, then unfold.

3. Fold along this blue line and press down so the corner meets the central dot.

7. Fold along this green line, then press down so the glued areas stick.

6. Add glue to this shaded area.

5. Add glue to this shaded area.

CUT HERE!

© MGA

A letter to my future self.
Open when you ____ years old.

WORDS OF WISDOM

The L.O.L. babes want to inspire you to believe in yourself and follow your dreams! Color in the words of wisdom below and come back to this page anytime you need a lil' L.O.L. encouragement.

Inspire

BELIEVE

STRENGTH

Dream

Courage

CONFIDENCE

LOVELY LETTERS

Everyone likes receiving letters – especially your BFFs! Use the notepaper on the following pages to write letters to your friends. Want to keep your letters extrasecret? Follow the instructions below to fold your letters into a totally adorbs heart shape!

YOU WILL NEED:
- Scissors
- A pen or pencil to write with

REMEMBER!
ASK AN ADULT TO HELP YOU

Top Tip
WHEN FOLDING YOUR LETTERS, MAKE SURE YOU START WITH THE WORDS FACEUP AND THE PATTERN FACEDOWN. THAT WAY, YOUR FOLDED CREATIONS WILL LOOK SUPERCUTE AND YOUR LETTER WILL BE KEPT EXTRASECRET!

Steps:

1. Ask an adult to help you cut out your letter.

2. Place your letter with the pattern side down and the words facing you.

3. Fold the top right corner downwards so that it meets the left side of the paper. Unfold, and do the same thing to the left corner. Do not unfold.

4. Fold the bottom part of the paper in half, so that the bottom edge of your paper meets the bottom edge of the folded section. The words of your letter shouldn't show anymore.

© MGA

5. Unfold the top part of the paper and turn it over. You should now have two diagonal creases on the paper.

6. Fold the top part of the paper down so that the fold crosses through the middle of the two diagonal creases, then unfold.

7. Turn the paper over again. Take the left and right sides of the paper (where the horizontal crease is) and pull them towards the center of the paper. As you pull them, the other two creases should be folding, too. Pull the two sides inwards so they touch and then press the top of the paper down.

8. Fold the bottom left corner of the triangle so that it meets the top point. Only fold the top layer of paper. Make the same fold on the right side. You should now have a diamond shape.

9. Fold the sides over towards the center to meet up with the bottom sides of the diamond.

10. Fold the paper in half vertically, then unfold. Turn the paper over.

11. Take the two bottom corners and fold them up to meet at the center.

12. Fold the large triangular flap at the top downwards. Tuck the two bottom corners into the space inside the folded flap.

13. Fold the two top flaps downwards at an angle.

14. Tuck the corners of the two small flaps into the space inside the big flap beneath them.

15. Take a moment to admire your creation, then pass your secret note to your BFF.

Amazing work, B.B!